All About Me!

by Lesley E. Thompson

by Karen Anderson
illustrated by Christine Ross

Learning Media

Contents of My Awesome Project

me!

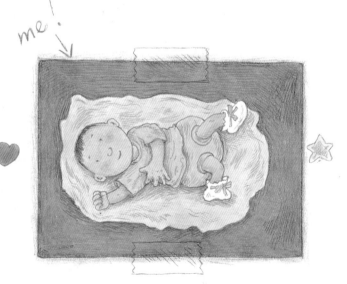

Dedicated to Miss Kimberley,
my awesome teacher.

Dear Miss Kimberley,

I thought I should tell you that Mom spilled her chocolate pudding on my project. That's why it has stains on it.

From,

Lesley E. Thompson

1.
My Family

My name is Lesley E. Thompson.
I'm eight years old. This is a project
about some of the things that have
happened to me.

Here's a photo of me. My teeth are sticking out, but I still think I look quite cute.

Here's a photo of my big brother. His ears aren't really as big as dinner plates. And he doesn't really wear thick glasses. My best friend, Stinky, made me draw him like this.

Here's a photo of Mom and Dad on their wedding day. Who do you think I look like?

2.
When I Was Small

Here's a photo of Mom with me inside her tummy. I don't remember much about being in there.

Here's a photo of me outside Mom's tummy. I have just seen my big brother for the very first time.

This is me when I first learned to walk. I tipped over all the houseplants. I thought they would be good to hold onto, but I was wrong.

I'm two years old in this photo. I'm playing with my cat, Stretch, and our dog, Roger. Roger and I had lots of adventures chasing Stretch around the house.

3.
My Best Friend, Stinky

Stinky's real name is Susie, but I call her Stinky. That's because when she was six, she didn't take a bath for a whole week.

She made splashing sounds with her hands in the bathtub. This fooled her mom for six days. But the next day her mom came into the bathroom, and Stinky got caught. Her mom was so mad!

I was the one who taught Stinky how to eat dirt from houseplants. In fact, I've taught Stinky just about everything she knows. I'm real proud of that.

Here I am at my fourth birthday party. I'm crying because my brother put chocolate in my hair. That was after I'd put a cupcake on his chair.

This is me and Stinky when we wanted
to be astronauts. Stinky used Mom's
best vase for her space helmet.
That goldfish in the jar is Eric.

Here's Mom picking up me and
Stinky after our first day at
Kindergarten. I really liked painting
time. I didn't know what to paint. The
teacher said, "Why don't you paint
your friend?" So I did!

Here's another photo from Kindergarten.
The boy beside me is Steven.

Stinky told Steven that play dough tasted like double chocolate ice cream. Steven believed her. He ate all of the yellow and the blue play dough. No wonder he looks green!

4.
How My Life Nearly Ended

Here I am on vacation with my family. Can you *see* that tree in the background? I climbed right to the top ... then I fell!

I cut my head open when I hit the ground. Ouch! It hurt! I got a cut that needed eight stitches.

Dad was sitting under the tree reading. I just about landed on top of him. Dad nearly fainted when he saw my cut.

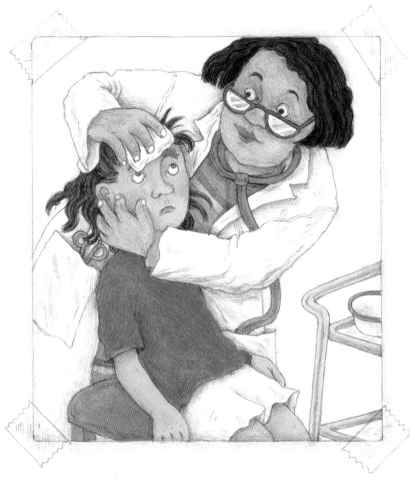

Mom took me to the hospital. The doctor asked me how I had hurt myself. "My big brother was being kidnapped by a pirate," I told her. "The pirate slashed me with his sword."

Mom looked real worried. She put her hand on my forehead to see if I had a fever. My brother poked his tongue out at me. The doctor didn't ask any more questions after that.

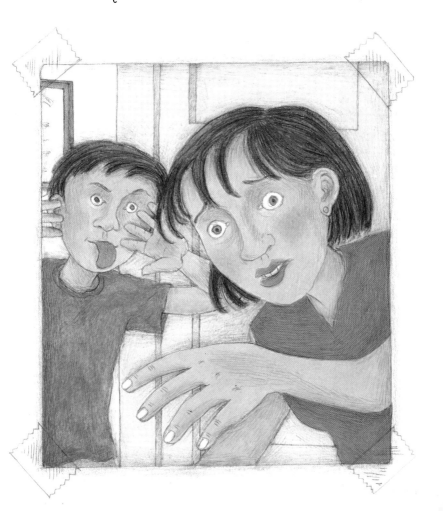

5.
In the Future

This is my family now. Mom has grown quite a lot because she has three babies inside her. Triplets! I can hardly believe it.

They'll be born any day now. I want to teach them everything I know. I told Dad this, and he looked real worried. I don't know why he's so worried. I've turned out OK, haven't I?

I told Dad that one day I'll be president. Then I can make up some new rules to make life easier for the triplets and for other kids too.

Dad just laughed and patted me on the head, but he'll see!

Rules I Will Make When I Am President

1. Weekends will last for five days, and school will last for two days.

2. All kids will get fifty dollars pocket money each week.

3. Kids will not have to do chores to earn their pocket money.

4. Kids can eat whatever they want to eat.

5. All kids will have these things in their bedroom:

- a phone
- a TV
- a computer with the Internet
- a soda machine.

6. Kids can go to bed whenever they want to.

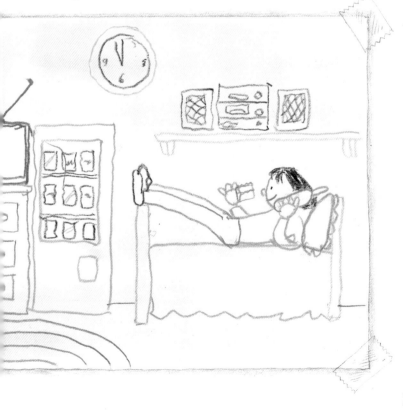

I have left this page blank for comments from my very pretty teacher who is never mad and is always smiling.

Lesley

Grade: A

I like your idea about school only being two days a week. Please let me know if there is anything I can do to help you be elected as president.

Miss Kimberley